CARNY GAMES 2

A SEX PARTY

JADE'S EROTIC ADVENTURES
BOOK 50

VICTORIA RUSH

VOLUME 50

JADE'S EROTIC ADVENTURES - BOOK 50

COPYRIGHT

ALSO BY VICTORIA RUSH

Adult Fairytales:

The Enchanted Forest: An Erotic Fairytale

The Land of Giants: An Erotic Fairytale

The Dragon's Lair: An Erotic Fairytale

Witch's Brew: An Erotic Fairytale

The Mage's Spell: An Erotic Fairytale

The Mermaid Lagoon: An Erotic Fairytale

The Coven: An Erotic Fairytale

Rapunzel: An Erotic Fairytale

The Seven Dwarfs: An Erotic Fairytale

The Land of Mutants: An Erotic Fairytale

The Erotic Temple: A Sexy Fairytale (Coming Soon)

Erotica Themed Bundles:

Voyeur: Lesbian Erotica Bundle

Public Affairs: A Lesbian Anthology

Futa Fantasies: The Ladyboy Collection

Threesomes: The Lesbian Collection

Threesomes - Volume 2: The Lesbian Collection

First Time: A Lesbian Anthology

Hedonism: An Erotic Anthology

Switch Hitters: Bisexual Erotica

Taboo Erotica: The Lesbian Series

BDSM: The Lesbian Collection

Party Games: The Erotic Collection

Party Games 2: The Erotic Collection

All Girl 1: Lesbian Erotica Bundle

All Girl 2: Lesbian Erotica Bundle

All Girl 3: Lesbian Erotica Bundle

All Girl 4: Lesbian Erotica Bundle

Erotic Fairytale Bundles:

Clover's Fantasy Adventures: Books 1 - 5

Clover's Fantasy Adventures: Books 6 - 10

Erotic Fantasy:

Pirate's Bounty: A Time Travel Adventure

Wild West: A Time Travel Adventure

Private Riley: A Time Travel Adventure

Cleopatra's Secret: A Time Travel Adventure

Bounty Hunter 2125: A Time Travel Adventure

Ninja Assassin: A Time Travel Adventure

The 300: A Time Travel Adventure

Arabian Nights: An Erotic Fairytale (coming soon...)

Steamy Time Travel Bundles:

Riley's Time Travel Adventures: Books 1 - 5

Lesbian Erotica:

The Dinner Party: Lesbian Voyeur Erotica

The Darkroom: Bisexual Voyeur Erotica

Naked Yoga: Lesbian Transgender Erotica

Nude Cruise: Bisexual Voyeur Erotica

Rush Hour: Taboo Public Sex

The Girl Next Door: First Time Lesbian Erotic Romance

Girls' Camp: Lesbian Group Sex

Wet Dream: Ladyboy Fantasy Erotica

The Convent: Taboo Sex with a Nun

Sex Robot: A Dream Sex Machine

The Personal Trainer: Getting Pumped at the Gym

The Dominatrix: BDSM Lesbian Domination

Webcam Chat: Lesbian Online Sex

Paint Me: A Kinky Bodypainting Workshop

The Toy Party: Girls Sharing Sex Toys

The Costume Party: Strapping One On

Swedish Sauna: Lesbian Group Sex

The Therapist: Taboo Lesbian Erotica

Elevator Shaft: Bisexual Threesomes Erotica

Ladyboy: Lesbian Transgender Erotica

Peep Show: Lesbian Voyeur Erotica

The Dare: Public Sex Erotica

Maid Service: Lesbian Threesomes Erotica

The Hitchhiker: First Time Lesbian Erotica

The Housesitter: Spycam Lesbian Erotica

The Spa: Lesbian Group Orgy

Parlor Games: Blindfold Sex Party

The Exchange Student: First Time Lesbian Erotica

The Hostel: Bisexual Group Erotica

The Harem: Lesbian Erotic Romance

The Orient Express: Lesbian Voyeur Erotica

The First Lady: A Forbidden Lesbian Erotic Romance

The Slave: Lesbian BDSM Erotica

The Masseuse: Lesbian Sensuous Erotica

Too Close for Comfort: Lesbian Forbidden Erotica

Naked Twister: A Wild Party Game

Lexi: The Sex App (Lesbian Fantasy Erotica)

Call Girl: Lesbian Bisexual Threesomes Erotica

Circle Jill: Lesbian Masturbation Workshop

The Viewing Room: Masturbation Voyeur Erotica

Spin the Bottle: A Kinky Party Game

The Hair Salon: Lesbian Voyeur Erotica

Tribadism 1: Girls Only Sex Workshop

Tribadism 2: The Art of Scissoring

Tribadism 3: Threeway Hookups

The Kiss: A Game of Oral Sex

Pledge Week: Sorority Sisters

Carny Games 1: A Wild Sex Party

Carny Games 2: A Kinky Sex Party

Carny Games 3: An Erotic Sex Party

Dreamscape: An Artificial Reality Game

Glory Hole: Guess Who's On the Other Side

Joy Ride: A Late Night Erotic Bus Trip

The Blind Girl: An Erotic Romance(Coming Soon)

Lesbian Erotica Bundles:

Jade's Erotic Adventures: Books 1 - 5

Jade's Erotic Adventures: Books 6 - 10

Jade's Erotic Adventures: Books 11 - 15

Jade's Erotic Adventures: Books 16 - 20

Jade's Erotic Adventures: Books 21 - 25

Jade's Erotic Adventures: Books 26 - 30

Standalone Stories:

The Polynesian Girl: A Lesbian EroticRomance

For the uninhibited...

WANT TO AMP UP YOUR SEX LIFE?

Sign up for my newsletter to receive more free books and other steamy stuff. Discover a hundred different ways to wet your whistle!

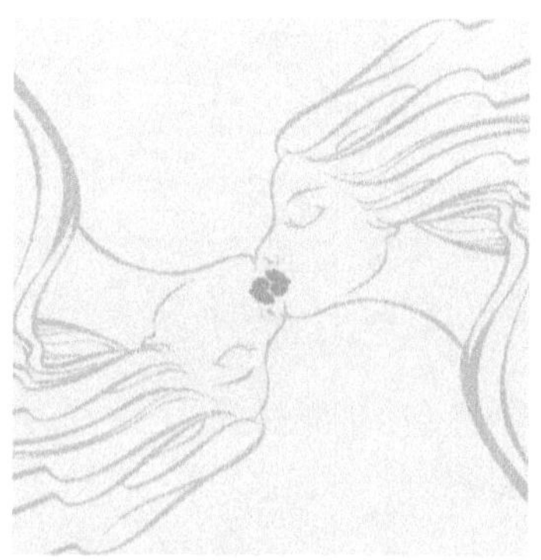

Victoria Rush Erotica

1

———

After the last game where we watched Shae spurting while she rode the Sybian machine to orgasm, I was excited to discover what the next contest would be. Madison had alternated the focus of each game between the men and the women, and watching the guys' still-bobbing dicks dripping strings of cum from their flaring heads was getting me even more worked up thinking about it.

"That was crazy-hot," I said. "But from the look of things, I think the boys are eager to see what's in store for them in the next round."

"Funny you should ask," Maddy smiled, reaching behind her to reach into her game kit behind the sofa. "Because I've been looking forward to this next contest ever since I came up with the idea for this party."

She lifted her hand, clutching a cluster of pink plastic rings.

"In this next version of the classic carnival game *Ring Toss*, the ladies will be aiming at something a little more interesting than Coke bottles. That is, if the boys can stay hard long enough to let the women claim their prize."

"I dunno," Brad's wife Laura said, glancing at her husband's flagging erection. "After that last exhibition, I'm not sure how much more energy the guys have left. Some of them have come three times already."

"I suppose that depends on what the *prize* is," Brad grinned, grabbing his dripping tool and trying to bring his hard-on back to life.

"Just like with the previous contests," Madison nodded. "Each winner will have a chance to hook up with their partner."

"How do we decide who's the *winner*?" the sexy redhead, Paige, said.

"Each of the ladies will be given five plastic rings," Madison continued. "While the men line up side-by-side, the women will toss their rings toward their opposing partner. The one who lands the most rings on their partner's penis, wins."

Lincoln furrowed his brow, squinting at the narrow hoops in Madison's hand.

"Are you sure those rings are *large* enough?" he said. "Because it seems to me that those of us who are, er, a little better endowed, are at a distinct disadvantage in this game."

Madison peered at Linc's thick pole and raised herself up off the sofa with a devilish grin on her face.

"Why don't we *test* it to make sure?"

She slipped one of the rings over the tip of his hard-on, sliding it slowly up and down his long shaft.

"Seems to fit well enough," she said. "What you may be losing in wider girth should be more than counterbalanced by your longer length. You'll be that much closer to your partner while she aims for your dick."

Shae shuffled her feet impatiently while she watched Madison place a line of masking tape on the floor a few feet in front of the fireplace.

"Which side of the line do you want *me* to be on this time?" she said. "I seem to qualify on both sides."

"I'll leave that up to you," Madison smiled.

"Frankly, I could use a bit of a rest," Shae said, licking her lips while she appraised the lineup of rising dicks as the men took positions in front of the fireplace. "Besides, I'm kind of hungry for a *different* kind of treat this time."

"Alright then, ladies," Madison said, watching the men standing cheek-to-cheek with their hard-ons bobbing in front of their stomachs. "Choose a partner and assume your position. Each of you will be given five rings, which you'll toss directly toward your opposing player. Anyone who steps over the line will be immediately disqualified."

The women scrambled to the front of the line, bumping against one another as they fought to claim their preferred position. Madison grinned when she saw that Laura had chosen to lineup opposite the handsome Latino, Diego, instead of her husband, also noticing that Shae had quickly positioned herself in front of Linc. While the rest of the women smiled at their chosen partners, she handed out the rings to each of the contestants, then she moved to the side of the line to act as referee.

"Is everybody ready?" she said.

"It looks like it didn't take long for the guys to recover their stamina," I chuckled, glancing at Brad's erection tapping against the front of his stomach while he peered back at me.

"What's good for the goose is good for the gander," he grinned, winking at his wife, who was staring at Diego as she licked her lips.

"Alright then," Madison nodded. "Gentlemen, start your engines."

Each of the women leaned forward as far as they could without stepping over the line, then they tossed their rings toward their partners' erections, bouncing off their dicks and onto the floor.

"No fair!" Laura protested, watching the rings bouncing on the floor. "This contest is rigged, just like the one at the county fair. The rings are too small to fit over the targets!"

"It doesn't appear to be a problem for *Lincoln and Shae*," Maddy smiled, nodding toward the couple at the far end of the line.

Laura turned to peer in their direction and frowned when she saw Shae's first ring resting on Linc's big cock half way down his shaft.

"It's obviously not a *size* issue," Madison said. "It looks to be more a matter of technique."

"Hmm," Laura said, glowering at Diego while his dick flapped in front of his stomach. "Stop *moving* while I try to lasso that bobbing prick."

"It's not as easy as it looks," Diego replied. "This thing has a mind of its own."

Everybody laughed, then the women leaned forward again, pausing as they took aim at the men's fluttering penises. This time a few more rings landed on their targets while the other women groaned watching their rings fall onto the floor.

"You're not leaving me much room to snare your dick," I said, peering at Brad's erection pressed up against his stomach.

"I can't help it," he said. "It's *always* like this when I'm this turned on."

I glanced to the end of the line where Shae stood grinning while she stared at Linc's purple prick, standing proudly at attention with two pink rings encircling his shaft.

"Well, *somebody* seems to have found the secret to landing these things. Just do whatever Lincoln's doing. Otherwise, those two are going to be having all the fun once again when this contest is over."

"Okay," Brad said, bending forward a few degrees, trying to present an easier target.

This time, some of the women tilted their heads toward Lincoln and Shae before they threw their next ring, noticing Linc jutting his hips forward and gripping the base of his pole to angle it in Shae's direction.

"They're cheating!" Bonnie said, flaring her eyes at Madison. "He's using his *hand* to help capture the ring!"

"Nobody said you couldn't use other parts of your anatomy," Maddy grinned. "As long as you don't move your feet, you're welcome to do whatever you can to win the contest. You wouldn't hold still while someone tried to throw a piece of *popcorn* into your mouth, would you?"

"*Now* you tell us," I huffed, peering toward Brad.

He grasped his shaft and bent it down a few inches, and this time my ring landed on the tip of his pole, sliding off the slippery crown and bouncing onto the floor.

"Wipe your pre-cum off the tip of your cock," I scolded him. "That extra lubrication isn't helping things."

Laura suddenly leaned over, glancing at her husband's glistening tool.

"Are you getting *excited* about the prospect of fucking another contestant, sweetheart?" she teased.

"After my *last* hookup, I'm ready to take my chances with somebody of the opposite sex," Brad smiled.

"So am I," Laura said, grinning at Diego, who nodded

excitedly as he peered down at her last ring encircling his pole.

For the next couple of rounds, each of the couples paused to line up their targets while the men used their hands to angle their pricks in the direction of the rings, but after the final disk had been tossed, the winner was plain to see. When Madison stepped forward to inspect the men's penises, Lincoln's huge penis had four rings attached to it while Diego and Marco had two, and most of the others only had one.

"It looks like size *does* matter in this instance," Madison grinned, flapping Lincoln's cock to the side as the rings jostled loudly on his flaring dick. "It seems that you two are going to be the center of attention once again while the rest of the contestants stand back and watch."

2

———

"Have you thought about how you'd like to engage with your partner this time, Shae?" Madison said.

"Are you kidding me?" Shae smiled. "I've been dreaming about what I'd like to do with this python ever since I saw it unsheathed in the first round."

"It looks like you've got a few more options than most," Maddy chuckled, peering down at her engorged penis and dripping pussy.

"Can I use *all* of them?" Shae said.

Madison paused for a moment, then shook her head.

"In the interest of sharing the spoils, I think it's only fair that you use one part at a time. I'm pretty sure there are a few *other* guests that would like to take a turn with you. Besides, the party isn't even half over, and the clock's ticking for our next contest. Why don't you two put on a little show while the rest of us fantasize about what's coming next?"

Shae smiled and took a step toward Linc, slapping the side of her cock against his like she was sword fighting.

"Well, if it's a *show* they want," she said. "Maybe we

should let it all hang out this time. Are you up for a little *cock play*, Lincoln? I know you said you don't swing that way, but if you're doing it with somebody with *tits*, it's not really gay, is it?"

Lincoln hesitated while he peered down at Shae's throbbing hard-on, slowly sliding his gaze up her body, pausing at her bouncing tits and rosebud lips.

"With you, I'm prepared to do just about *anything*," he smiled.

"Sit down on the floor and spread your legs then," Shae said while she rubbed her fingers over the tip of his dripping crown. "Because it's about to get interesting."

Lincoln sat down on the floor and bent his knees, propping his arms behind his back while his long erection bobbed between his legs. Shae sat down in a similar manner, facing him as she slowly pulled the plastic rings off his glistening dick one at a time.

"Mmm," she purred, gazing into his eyes while she paused near the tip of his prick, twisting each ring around the sensitive flesh under the frenulum. "Maybe I'll get a chance to slide something *else* over this beautiful tool before this night is over. It's a shame to leave so much of this organ to waste."

"Just say the word and I'll be happy to dip it into your pool," Lincoln said, meeting Shae's gaze with a pearly smile.

"It's tempting," she smiled back at him. "But right now, I want to feel your manhood pounding against *another* part of my anatomy."

After she lifted the last of the rings off his cock, she shimmied her hips forward, pressing the underside of her hard-on against Linc's upturned pole, gripping both of their instruments with two hands.

"Fuck, yes," Shae groaned. "That's what I'm talking

about. Do you like the feeling of our cocks pressed together?"

"Yes," Linc panted. "It feels so–*warm.*"

"And *slippery*," Shae smiled. "You're dripping like a fountain over your monument."

"So are you," Linc said, peering between their legs at the puddle of fluid accumulating between Shae's legs.

"That's the advantage of being a *real* ladyboy," Shae grinned. "I get to fuck you with my outer part while I lubricate us with my inner part."

"Yes," Lincoln groaned. "Rub my dick with your pretty girl-cock. I want to watch you spray your cum all over my chest."

"That makes two of us," Shae said, leaning forward to kiss Lincoln while she slid her cock against his, gripping their dicks tightly in her hands.

"Mfft," Linc grunted as he felt Shae's tits sliding against his muscular chest.

He wrapped his arms around her back and pulled her closer to him, thrusting his hips more rapidly in her hands. The sensation of his dick sliding against her burning organ while his balls rubbed against her dripping pussy only added to the excitement of his first-time encounter with a transgender partner.

While the rest of us looked on from the edge of the sofa, we rubbed our own dripping genitals as we stared silently at the erotic scene unfolding before us. While Lincoln and Shae amped up the intensity of their muffled humping and moaning, each of us began to feel our own orgasms building toward an inexorable climax.

"Fuck, yes," Lincoln groaned into Shae's mouth. "Grip my dick harder with your hands. I want to feel you pulsing against me when you come. I'm getting closer..."

"Yes, baby," Shae hummed. "Let it go. Squirt all over my tits while you come in my hands. Your cock feels so hot..."

"Yes, yes, yes," Lincoln huffed as the tips of his fingers dug into Shae's back. "That feels so good. Oh God, here it comes–"

Suddenly, he lifted Shae's body off the floor as he tilted her pussy onto the base of his dick while he thrust his hips hard into her hands one last time, jetting a long string of ropes onto her belly and tits while he thrashed and groaned on the floor, moaning into her mouth. When Shae's cock began squirting soon after, the entire room erupted in a cacophony of squeals and moans, with the rest of us unable to resist our own overflowing pleasure any longer.

While I squirted my own juices over Madison's leather sofa, I glanced over at her, noticing she'd removed the last of her clothing, with the fingers of two hands deeply embedded in her pussy, shaking uncontrollably along with the rest of us.

We're going to have to find another way to get her involved in the action, I thought to myself, catching her eye as we convulsed together in mutual ecstasy.

3

———————

"Whew!" Madison said after everybody came down from their powerful climaxes. "Why don't we take a break so everyone can clean up and recharge with a little nourishment? There's plenty of wine and beer in the fridge and some hors d'oeuvres on the kitchen table."

"What's up next?" Lily asked. "Isn't it the *girls'* turn for some fun in the next round?"

"Right you are, Lily," Madison nodded. "But I'd rather keep it a surprise until everyone regroups. All I can say is I guarantee you'll be dripping *wet* by the time we finish the next round."

Everybody retired to the kitchen and milled around the large island while we noshed on cheese tarts and pita with tzatziki. By now, we'd all lost any reservations about prancing around naked, having already been exposed in the most intimate settings. When Lincoln and Shae entered the room after cleaning up, everybody grinned at them, clapping loudly.

"That was fucking hot," I said to Shae as she nudged in next to me, helping herself to a generous serving of tzatziki.

"Tell me about it," Shae nodded. "I think Lincoln sprayed more jizz on me than this whole bowl of tzatziki."

"I wouldn't doubt it," I laughed. "With that giant poker and cannon balls, I'm sure he's storing more than his fair share."

"So what do you think Madison's planning next?" she said. "Each game seems to be getting wilder and crazier than the one before."

"I don't know, but based on how hard she came watching you and Linc go at, she must be almost as eager as the rest of us to resume the festivities."

"It's too bad we can't get her more involved in the action," Shae nodded. "It doesn't seem fair for her to stand back as a spectator for each of the contests."

"We'll have to see if we can switch roles somewhere along the way," I said. "Not every game needs a referee, and I'm sure she'd love to be on the receiving end of some of the games."

"Or the *giving* end," Shae smiled.

"Let's see what this next contest involves," I nodded. "With the focus returning to the girls, there should be plenty of opportunity for her to get more involved."

When we returned to the living room, I noticed the furniture had been rearranged with the sofa set back a further distance from the fireplace and set perpendicular to the opposing wall. Madison had draped a waterproof tarp over the edge of the hearth, and in her hand she held a clutch of brightly colored panties.

"What's all this?" I said. "It looks like you're getting ready for some kind of *flood*."

"Well, there'll be water involved," Maddy grinned. "But with any luck, it'll be concentrated in a small area so as not to make too much of a mess."

"What's with the colorful panties?" Shae said. "Just when we were beginning to get comfortable running around naked."

Madison raised one of the panties and spread it apart, revealing a patch of concentric circles woven into the crotch.

"In this next contest I'll call *Bullseye*, the boys are going to be taking their turn shooting water pistols at your pussies. Kind of like in the carnival game where you shoot pellets at a paper target, the challenge will be to soak the targeted area in the allotted time."

"Do we have to soak the *entire* bullseye?" Ryan said, peering at the large red circles on the front of the garment.

"Yes," Madison nodded. "I'll be inspecting each set of panties upon completion to see if the full outer ring is darkened."

"How much time will we have?" Diego said.

"Three minutes."

"And we'll be firing from the edge of the sofa?" Brad said.

"Exactly."

"That doesn't sound so hard," Marco huffed.

"It *will* be, when you're using a small water pistol with limited water storage," Madison said.

She grabbed a bucket of water and placed it in front of the sofa, then reached into her game kit to hand each of the men a plastic pistol.

"Where do you want me to sit this time?" Shae said.

"Why don't you take a turn with the *boys* for a change?"

Madison smiled. "Your pecker might be a bit of an unnecessary distraction for your opposing partner."

"That's too bad," Shae laughed. "I was kind of hoping I could act as referee this round so we could get *you* more involved in the action."

"You might be able to twist my arm for the contest coming up in a couple of rounds," Madison said. "This one's pretty simple, but it will still require a discerning eye."

"What's the prize for the winner?" Lincoln said.

"Same as always," Maddy nodded. "Another hook-up with your opposing partner."

"Will there be any limitations on what we're allowed to do with each other this time?" Lincoln asked.

"You can do whatever your partner wants. Although she'll likely be pretty worked up by the time you finish the contest. You better be ready to dive in as soon as we announce the winner."

"Oh, I'll be ready to *dive in*, alright," Lincoln grinned, peering at the women's glistening pussies while Madison handed out the panties. "I'm ready to sink my sword to the *hilt* this time."

"I wouldn't get your hopes up too high," Madison nodded, glancing at his rising organ. "This time it's going to be a pretty level playing field."

4

———

After each of the women pulled on their bullseye panties and took up positions on the edge of the hearth, the men sat down side-by-side on the sofa, dipping their water pistols into the bucket to fill their reservoirs and lining up their partner's pussies through the gun sights.

Laura flapped her knees apart while she grinned at her husband, who'd chosen to line up directly opposite her position on the hearth.

"It shouldn't be so hard for you to find the magic spot this time," she teased, peering down at the bullseye between her legs.

"Maybe we should wear these more often," Lily nodded, adjusting the center of the bullseye over the base of her mound. "It's pretty hard to miss the clit with these bright red circles pointing directly to the target."

All the women chuckled, then they slowly spread their legs apart, revealing the titillating target of five pulsating pussies daring the men to soak their snatches. I was happy to have the handsome Hispanic hunk, Diego, as my counterpart this time, and I winked at him while he raised his pistol, awaiting Maddy's start signal. As she raised her arm and prepared to start the timer, I could already feel my panties dampening anticipating his teasing of my private parts.

When she lowered her arm and signaled for everyone to start, a volley of water jets squirted in our direction, spraying each of us all over our bodies. While we blinked our eyes and spat out the water splattering over our tits and faces, we laughed out loud at the men's clumsiness.

"Come on, boys," Paige teased, wiping the drops off her melon-sized tits. "Surely you can do better than that. Even my high-school boyfriend got to second base faster than that."

"It's not for want of trying," Marco huffed, shaking his head as he took aim again. "These pistols have crappy aim. It's going to take a little practice to adjust our targets."

"That's what they all say," Bonnie chuckled.

The men refocused their aim, holding their pistols with two hands while they lined up their partner's bullseyes, and this time most of the volleys landed closer to the women's hips. I felt Diego's next shot land just below my belly button, and I tilted my hips upward, feeling the trickle dribble down over my clit. As crazy as this concept was, I found it highly stimulating to have my partner shooting water jets at my pussy, and before long, my own lubrication began to dampen the cloth between my legs as much as Diego's increasingly accurate shots.

After a few more volleys, some of the men's pistols ran out of water, and they hastily dipped them back into the bucket to refill them, desperately trying to finish soaking their partner's bullseye before time ran out. I peered down at my crotch and noticed the outer rings had begun to darken from Diego's sure aim, but the inner circle still remained clean and dry.

"Shoot a little higher," I encouraged Diego. "Aim for my clit, and I'll help do the rest."

"One minute left!" Madison called out, glancing at the timer counting down on her phone screen. "You guys better speed up the pace, or we might not have *any* winner this round."

Diego nodded when he heard my coaching, and I lifted my hips a few inches off the hearth, feeling my pussy beginning to buzz in excitement. When his next two volleys caught me square on my button, I moaned in pleasure, feeling a sense of urgency building up inside me.

"Yes, Diego," I panted, noticing my wet spot beginning to spread in my panties. "Keep hitting me right there. That feels so good. You're going to make me come soon if you keep doing it like that."

"Mmm," Diego nodded, his cock starting to rise between his legs when he realized the effect he was having on me. "Who cares about *winning* when the process of getting there is so exciting? I haven't had this much fun since I spied on my middle-grade classmates through the girls' locker room window."

"If you finish the job, I'll give you more than just a *peek* at my pussy," I grinned, feeling my pleasure growing stronger with each pulse of his water pistol upon my gland. "I'm getting close..."

Just as Madison called the time and signaled for everyone to stop, Diego's last volley jetted hard against my clit, and I suddenly shuddered, feeling my juices gushing out of my pussy, soaking the entire crotch of my panties. While Madison began to walk down the line inspecting each of the women's panties, I shook silently, enjoying my quiet orgasm while Diego nodded at me knowingly. By now, his cock was standing at full attention as he caressed the glistening tip, watching me staring back at him with my mouth half-agape.

When Madison reached my position at the end of the line, she peered down at my panties and smiled.

"It appears that we have a winner," she nodded. "Though from the look of things, I think Diego may have had a little help from the opposite side of the range. Jade's panties are soaked all the way through. Somebody seemed to enjoy that more than the many of us expected."

Then she peered back at Diego and smiled.

"Are you ready to claim your prize, Diego?"

"Damn straight," Diego said, standing up and displaying his rock-hard erection angled up over his tight balls. "How would you like me to do this?" he said, approaching me with a sexy flush on his face.

"Just *take* me," I panted. "I've already come. I just want to feel you inside me."

"You don't have to ask twice," Diego said, kneeling down in front of me and pushing my legs apart while he tore off the patch in front of my crotch.

When he saw my dripping vulva exposed in the hole of my panties, he grabbed the sides of my ass and pulled me close to him, inserting his tool deep into my crevice. I grunted when I felt him penetrate me, then I wrapped my arms and legs around his body as he pounded me against the fireplace with everybody staring at his flexing buttocks while he fucked me shamelessly. It barely took a minute for both of us to climax together while we shook in each other's arms with everybody nodding appreciatively.

While Madison stood on from a distance away, caressing her breasts softly with two hands, I glanced down at her parted legs, noticing a trickle of lubrication dripping down the inside of her thighs.

Damn girl, I thought. *This carnival game concept is fucking genius. It's almost as much fun watching the action as participating in it.*

Almost, I grinned. *Next time, it's your turn.*

5

———————

"Mmm," Madison said, emerging from the kitchen carrying a large bowl after Diego and I recovered from our orgasms. "That was positively *delicious!*"

The bowl was filled with some kind of fluffy pink material that looked like spun cotton.

"Speaking of delicious," she said, lifting a wooden ladle out of the bowl, covered in cotton candy. "What county fair is complete without a *candy floss* treat?"

"Okay..." Shae said, squinting her eyes at the fluffy concoction. "Is this another one of your special *hors d'oeuvres*?"

"I guess you could look at it that way," Madison smiled. "But I had something a little more titillating in mind for its use. It's the boys' turn to be on the receiving end of the action this time, and I thought it would be a little more exciting if you licked it off their *penises* instead of just a cardboard stick."

Everybody's eyes widened, then Ryan shifted uncomfortably.

"Won't that be a little *messy*?" he said.

"Yes, I suppose so," Madison grinned. "But isn't that what makes these carnival games all the more interesting? The more mess we make, the more fun we all seem to have."

"Is this going to be another *contest* of some kind?" Lincoln said.

"Yes," Madison said, glancing at his oversized organ. "But this time I think you'll find your special endowments are more of a liability than an advantage. Because the winner will be the one who can lick all the candy floss off their partner's dick in the least time."

Laura suddenly laughed, shaking her head.

"Where do you come up with these ideas?" she said. "I mean, if the regular county fair had even *half* of these games, they'd sell out overnight."

"What can I say?" Madison grinned. "Sometimes I've got nothing better to do on lonely nights than dream up kinky sex games."

"It's pretty *kinky*, alright," Brad chuckled. "It's a good thing you told us to shave our private parts before we came to this party. Otherwise, we might have a hell of a time getting that stuff out of our pubic hair."

"Just another reason to stay clean and smooth," Madison nodded, noticing the men's dicks beginning to rise again at the thought of the women licking their tools.

"Can we choose our partners this time?" Ryan said, darting his eyes in Shae's direction.

"I don't see why not," Madison said.

"Can I choose *Shae* then, assuming she'll be on the women's side?"

"It's fine with me, as long as that works for Shae," Maddy nodded, glancing over at Shae.

"Absolutely," Shae smiled, peering at Ryan's hardening tool. "I can swing *both* ways, as it appears *Ryan* can too."

"Alright then," Madison said, motioning for the men to line up in front of the fireplace. "Let's get this party started."

"Do we have to be fully *hard* to do this?" Marco said, looking around self-consciously at some of the men's thickening cocks. "I mean, the less the women have to work with, the quicker they can complete the task."

"That may be true," Madison said. "But something tells me it'll be a helluva more fun for *both* of you if you're fully erect.

"And besides," she said, lifting the ladle out of the bowl and slathering a thick coating of sticky candy over Marco's tool. "By the time everyone's dicks are covered in cotton candy, it'll be hard to notice the difference."

By the time each of the women lined up in front of the men and Neil's penis had been coated in floss at the end of the line, I noticed all of the men's instruments standing proudly at attention. Even Marco's cock was jutting straight up now, as his partner Paige licked her lips, grinning up at him while she rested on her knees.

"Are you girls ready?" Madison said, holding her smartphone in her hand, ready to tap the timer.

"Not half as ready as the *men* seem to be," Laura chuckled, staring at Diego's candy-coated instrument flapping excitedly in front of her face.

"Alright then," Maddy smiled, preparing to tap the screen. "You'll have exactly three minutes to remove all traces of the candy from your partner's genitals. If there happens to be some *other* kind of residue left on their cocks by the time you're finished, we'll just consider that a bonus."

I peered down the line toward Laura, who'd chosen to line up opposite Lincoln.

"You better be careful cleaning that thing," I grinned. "If you're not careful, he'll poke your eye out."

"No worries," she winked, glancing up at Brad, whose erect penis was flapping hard against his belly, directly in front of me. "You just take care with my husband. Because from the look of things, he could pop off any second."

"Mmm," I said, licking my lips. "That will only make this treat all the more delicious."

When Madison signaled for everyone to start, the women began bobbing their heads and moving their faces from side to side as they hurried to remove the sticky cotton candy from their partners' genitals. While they sucked and licked with increasing urgency, the men moaned in rising unison, watching the women licking their tongues along the underside of their shafts and listening to the popping sound of their mouths plopping off their heads.

While I tried to grasp Brad's springy dick to gain better access to his top side, I glanced out the corner of my eye at Shae, who was sucking Ryan's cock like a porn star. She'd already removed most of the floss from around his shaft, and as she bobbed her head over his flaring crown, she rolled her hands around his balls, trying to remove the last vestiges of fluff. By the time I caught onto her technique and grabbed Brad's tool with both hands while I flicked his head with my tongue, Madison announced the end of the contest.

When the men groaned in disappointment at the early completion of the game, the women glanced down the line to compare their handiwork. The men's penises were still glistening and bouncing in excitement from their partner's attention, but each of them had traces of pink candy still encircling the base of their shafts and around their balls. Only Ryan's proud phallus shined clean and bright, his tight balls pulled up to the base of his flaring dick as he stared back at Shae's flushed face, still panting heavily. Madison walked down the line inspecting each man's junk, but it was obvious to everybody who had won the contest.

"I think you chose your partner wisely," Madison nodded when she reached the unlikely pair. "It seems that only someone who *owns* a cock knows how to properly suck another cock. It looks like Shae gave your balls just as much attention as your knob during that exercise."

"As every man should," Ryan smiled.

"Except I'm not a *man*," Shae huffed. "I might have a cock, but I'm just as much a woman as all the other ladies sitting here on their knees."

"I think we'd have to concur with that," Madison nodded. "It looks like you'll have your choice as to which side of the coin you'd like to avail yourself of in this case, Ryan. Have you thought about how you'd like to *finish* with your partner?"

"Mmm," Ryan hummed, staring down at Shae's big prick bobbing up between her legs. "As much as I enjoyed her expert *oral* attention, I've been wanting to feel that girl-cock inside me ever since I saw her rubbing dicks with Linc."

6

———

"Okay," Madison said, noticing a dribble of pre-cum leaking out of the tip of Shae's cock. "I'm sure everybody would love to have a bird's-eye view of the action, if you guys up for it. How can you position yourselves so we can enjoy the experience as much as the two of you?"

Shae paused for a moment peering up at Ryan, then she glanced at the fireplace, spreading a wide smile over her face.

"Why don't I rest on the hearth while you sit on my cock, facing away?" Shae said. "That way, you'll have maximum freedom of movement while I play with your cock from behind your back."

"Mmm," Ryan nodded. "And that will also be the perfect viewing position for the *rest* of the group."

"Works for me," I chuckled, imagining the sight of the two lovers fucking on the edge of the fireplace like two squatting frogs.

"Jeesuz," Paige said, flapping her hand in front of her face to signal how excited she was becoming. "Is it getting *hot* in here all of a sudden?"

"Not nearly as hot as it's *about* to be," Laura said, grabbing her husband's still bobbing cock and leading him over to the sofa for a prime viewing spot of the action.

"Why doesn't everybody line up boy-girl, boy-girl on the sofa so we can *all* enjoy the action equally?" Madison said, noticing both the men and the women squirming in anticipation of the show. "I'm sure the *rest* of the men are just as eager to get off as Ryan is after we ended the contest prematurely."

"Screw that," Bonnie chuckled. "I think the women are even *more* excited to watch this show. You guys might enjoy watching two women having sex, but we get just as turned on watching two guys go at it."

"Or in *this* case," I smiled, clarifying the terms of engagement. "A ladyboy and a gay boy."

"You heard the lady," Shae said to Ryan, sitting on the edge of the fireplace with her cock pointing straight up. "Sit on my dick, Ryan. Let's give these straight people a show they'll never forget."

Ryan paused for a moment, then he peered over at Madison.

"I don't suppose you've got any *lube* handy?" he said.

"Way ahead of you," Madison nodded, reaching into her game kit and tossing him a small purple bottle.

He peered at the label then squirted a dollop of jelly into his hands, rubbing it sensuously up and down Shae's throbbing hard-on.

"I'm not sure how much of this we actually need," he said, flaring his eyes at her dripping cock. "The combination of this lube mixed with Shae's jizz feels utterly sublime."

"Not as much as it will when I'm *inside* you," Shae groaned.

"Fuck, yes," Ryan said, spinning around and squatting over Shae's hips while she guided his pucker toward her hard-on.

When he felt the tip of her dick enter his sphincter, they both groaned while the rest of the gallery gasped watching her organ disappear inside his ass.

"Holy *fuck*," Laura hissed, watching their bodies rock together while she stroked Brad's sticky cock absent-mindedly beside her. "That's quite possibly the sexiest thing I've ever seen. Are you enjoying this as much as me, sweetheart?"

"I'm enjoying it, alright," Brad grunted, rocking his hips back and forth in his wife's hand. "But it would feel even better with a bit of extra lube."

Ryan glanced at the rest of the men sitting on the sofa next to their partners while they received their own hand jobs, then he reached down for the bottle of lube on the floor, tossing it gently toward Brad. He squirted a drop onto the top of his dick, then he passed it down the line while the rest of the men followed his lead. Within a few minutes, virtually everybody in the room was moaning and panting as they touched themselves and their partners while they watched the erotic scene unfolding only a few feet away.

Shae peered around the side of Ryan's stomach, and when she saw the rest of the women stroking their partner's cocks on the sofa, she reached around his hips and began stroking his erection while she squeezed his balls with her other hand.

"Fuck, that feels good," Ryan grunted, tensing his leg muscles as he bobbed up and down on Shae's flexing shaft.

"I bet you never knew it could be this much fun to fuck a *girl*, did you?" Shae joked, moaning in tandem with him.

The sight of her shiny dick sliding in and out of Ryan's ass while she pumped his darkening tool from behind was one of the sexiest things I'd ever witnessed. As they began to moan louder and louder in mutual pleasure, I stroked Neil's dick with my left hand while I jilled myself hard with my other hand. After a while, I noticed Madison standing slightly to my side near the edge of the sofa, quietly circling her clit while she watched the couple making out on the hearth, and I motioned for her to join me on the sofa. When she sat down next to me, I moved my right hand overtop of her pussy and slid my fingers into her slit, rolling my thumb over her hard clit. She placed her left hand over my pussy, and before long, everyone in the room was lost in the moment, enjoying the erotic show while they rubbed themselves closer to climax.

When Ryan began groaning with increased urgency and he lowered his ass all the way over Shae's glistening dick, we all watched with amazement while his hard-on erupted in a never-ending series of long squirts while Shae held him tightly with two hands. When his powerful spurts landed inches away from the base of the sofa, I listened to the rest of the group moaning along with Ryan and Shae, lost in the sweet symphony of the band of friends enjoying the shared experience of open-minded love.

7

———

"Wow," Madison said after everybody recovered from their powerful orgasms. "I don't know about the *rest* of you girls, but am I the *only* one who's feeling a twinge of penis envy?"

"That was pretty fucking hot," Paige nodded. "I wouldn't mind trying one of those on for a couple of days. There's something about the act of penetration that's kind of alluring..."

"That's why we *gay men* like to make use of every available orifice," Ryan smiled, raising up off Shae's dripping cock and wiping himself down with a nearby towel.

"And why we *hermaphrodites* are doubly blessed," Shae nodded, wiping down the insides of her thighs from her leaking pussy. "We get to experience it both ways."

"I *hate* you," I said, staring at Shae with a devilish grin.

"You can strap one on any time Jade, if you want to fuck me from behind," Shae chuckled.

"Speaking of cocks and fucking from behind," Madison interrupted. "I think our next contest might satisfy *everyone's* desire for penetration. In this variation of the game Pin the

Tail on the Donkey, we're going to try to pin our partner's ass with a something a little more interesting than just a floppy tail."

"You mean...?" Brad said, widening his eyes in excitement.

"That's right," Maddy nodded. "In this game, each of the men are going to try to complete the exercise by connecting their *cock* with their partner's ass."

"Blindfolded?" Lincoln said.

"Of course," Madison said. "Otherwise, it wouldn't be half as much fun."

"Who'll be the lucky girl on the receiving end?" I said. "If the men are all going to take a shot at the same target, doesn't that mean that only *one* woman will be involved this time?"

"So it would seem," Madison nodded. "Shall we draw lots to see who'll go first?"

Each of the women peered at one another for a moment, then we all turned together, staring at Madison.

"I think *Maddy* deserves a chance to participate in the game this time," I said. "Don't you agree, ladies?"

"Absolutely," Laura nodded. "She's obviously gotten just as turned on as the rest of us watching the action. It's only fair for her to have a turn."

"Plus, it doesn't look like there needs to be a *referee* to monitor the activity," Shae grinned. "It's going to be pretty obvious who'll be the winner."

"What do you say, Maddy?" I said, turning toward my friend. "Are you up for it?"

"You're twisting my arm," Madison chuckled. "Do you guys know how to play the game?"

"It's pretty simple, isn't it?" I said. "Each of the guys gets blindfolded one at a time, then we spin them around to disorient them a little, then they have to find their way to the target while we tell them if they're getting warmer or colder."

"Sounds about right," Madison nodded. "But to make it a little more challenging, you might place a few obstacles in their way to make it harder to find me."

"Like a chair or a footstool?" Emma said.

"Or maybe even another *person*," Maddy smiled. "Nothing works as well as a distraction like another person's naked body."

"Mmm," Paige nodded. "This is getting more interesting by the second."

"How long will each of us have to find you?" Marco said.

"I think about three minutes should be about right, given the size of the room," Madison grinned. "I'm not sure I can take six dicks up my ass if *everybody* wins."

"Is *that* where you want it if we win?" Lincoln said.

"I dunno," Madison said, looking at Linc's thick tool. "After that last demonstration with Ryan and Shae, I'm kind of intrigued to try it out. I'll leave it up to the winner to decide how he wants to connect with me. But in *your* case, Linc, you'd rip me apart if you tried going in the back door."

"You could be right about that," Lincoln chuckled. "I guess we'll just have to make it a surprise."

"Mmm," Maddy purred. "I like surprises."

"I suppose it's only fair that we blindfold *Madison* too, then," Shae said. "It's not like she's made it any easier for any of *us* so far."

"Works for me," Maddy nodded.

"Who'll be in charge of the timer?" Paige said.

"That depends on whether Shae wants to join the boys or the girls this time," Maddy smiled.

"I could use a bit of breather, to be honest," Shae sighed.

"After coming three times already, I need a couple of rounds to recover."

"Alright, then," Maddy said. "It looks like we're all set to go. Who's going to be our first candidate?"

"There doesn't seem to be an advantage going first or last in this case," Shae said, peering over at the men's swelling organs. "But based on who's got the hardest *tool* at this point, I'd have to give the nod to Brad."

Laura glanced at her husband's erect cock flapping up against his stomach and chuckled.

"I haven't seen you recover this fast from an orgasm in *ages*," she teased.

"What can I say?" Brad joked. "They say variety is the key to keeping your love life interesting. With so many willing partners at my disposal, this thing has a life of its own."

8

After everyone agreed on the rules of the game, Shae reached into Madison's game bag and tied a thick blindfold around Brad's eyes, spinning him around three times to disrupt his sense of direction. Then Madison tip-toed toward the kitchen, placing her hands over the edge of the island and bending over to reveal her shiny ass.

"Fucking eh," I sighed. "Maybe I'll strap on a dildo and give it a whirl too, if none of the guys manage to capture their prize. That's far too tempting a target to go to waste."

"You heard the lady," Shae said, tapping her smartphone to start the timer. "You've got exactly three minutes before the prize passes to someone else."

Brad raised his arms and began stepping gingerly in the opposite direction of Madison, and after a few seconds the viewing gallery began to hiss in unison.

"What does that mean?" he said. "Am I getting warmer or colder?"

"Colder," Emma said. "At this rate, Madison's pussy will *freeze over* before you reach her."

Brad stopped and turned around a hundred and eighty degrees, then he retracted his steps, heading toward the kitchen. When Laura saw that he was heading in the right direction, she jumped to her feet and scampered a few feet in front of him, standing rigidly like a statue. When he bumped into her, he groped her tits and ass, then his mouth widened with a lopsided smile.

"This figure feels familiar," he grinned. "And I'm pretty sure it's not Madison. Besides, she's not bending over like a *donkey*."

"Well, we can't make it *too* easy for you," Laura said, standing her ground. "You know how I always like to make you work for it. I'm afraid you won't come *back* to me if you sample too many of the goods tonight."

"Never fear, dear," Brad smiled. "My *cock* might be divining another source of opportunity, but my *heart* will always be true to you."

"Uh, huh," Laura huffed as he stepped around her and continued creeping toward the kitchen. She rushed back a few extra feet, pulling a large ottoman in his path, and Brad stumbled over it, falling onto the soft padding.

"You *really* don't want me fucking Maddy tonight, do you?" he grunted.

"I'm just trying to save your energy for the *next* contest," Laura grinned. "Madison always alternates the games between the boys and the girls, and I just want to make sure you'll be up for next opportunity."

"Don't worry, sweetheart," Brad said, picking himself up and beginning to walk toward the powder room. "I haven't felt this energized since I was a *teenager*. I'm pretty sure I'll be up for whatever Madison decides to throw at us."

He continued heading in the direction of the powder

room until he bumped his head against the door frame, lifting his hand to his forehead.

"You guys aren't going to make it any easier for me, are you?" he said, turning around and heading off in the direction of the dining room.

"Ssss..." the group hissed again, signaling that he was moving in the wrong direction.

He stopped and turned his head, trying to sense where Madison was hiding, but just as he began to head in the right direction, Shae announced that time was up.

"Shoot!" Brad said, tearing off his blindfold and watching Madison bending over the kitchen island teasingly, shaking her ass at him. "This is harder than it looks."

"Especially when your wife is *cock-blocking* you at every turn," Paige joked.

"Well, hopefully I'll have a chance to return the favor before the night is over," Brad said, returning to the sofa to sit beside the rest of the men, whose peckers were eagerly standing at attention, begging to be called next.

"Okay," Shae said, appraising the lineup of waving willies. "Who'd like to go next?"

"Shouldn't we blindfold Madison first, if we're going to keep it a secret?" I said, dipping into her kit bag and pulling out another bandana to place it around her head.

Shae paused to make sure she couldn't see anything, then she pointed toward Diego to go next. I led Madison by the arm into the adjacent living room, then hid her behind the big eight-person table before slapping her gently on the ass.

"Don't worry, babe," I said. "We'll get you properly hooked up before this contest is over."

"Can you try to give *Lincoln* a little head start?" she whispered to me. "I'd really like to feel his thumper up my ass if there's any way you can arrange it."

"I'll see what I can do," I chuckled, before returning quietly to the main group.

Each of the men tried their turn finding Madison in different areas of the lower level, but in each case, they bumped into various sundry obstacles, tripping and losing valuable time. When it finally became Lincoln's turn, he shook his head, doubting he'd ever capture the prize in time.

"I thought you girls said you wanted Madison to get her share of the spoils in this game?" he protested. "From the look of things, you're determined to deny her every chance."

"Have faith, Linc," I grinned. "Being last, you must have a pretty good sense of where the fixed objects are by now. Just follow your nose, and you'll get there eventually."

"Or your big *poker*," Shae laughed, wrapping the blind-fold around his eyes. As she spun him around, she stood teasingly close to his body, flapping his long hard-on from side-to-side while it slapped against her hips.

When she let him go, he crouched down a few inches, holding his hands out in front of him to locate the position of the surrounding furniture while the women gently coached him in the direction of Madison, who'd returned to her original location beside the kitchen island. As he twisted and turned closer and closer to her position, the women called out the words 'colder' or 'hotter', until he bumped up against her bent-over ass.

"Mmm," he said, holding out his hands to caress her buttocks. "This feels familiar. Although it's a lot softer and smoother than a *donkey*. Could this be the lovely hostess who's been tormenting us from one contest to another, making us jump through hoops and firing assorted objects at one another's private parts?"

"Possibly," Madison purred, reaching behind her to stroke his throbbing dagger. "Is this the hunk with a prick the size of a *horse*?"

"Possibly," Lincoln smiled, pressing the tip of his cock between her cheeks. "Do you have a preference for where you'd like me to connect my prize?"

"I think you'll find the *front* side a little more accommodating," Madison panted. "Not to mention wetter and warmer. I've been dripping like a *faucet* waiting for you to find me."

"Mmm," Lincoln said, grabbing the sides of Madison's ass and lifting her feet off the floor.

He tilted his dick up to her flaring hole, easing the tip of his thick organ into her glistening slit. When he pressed his hips forward and Madison felt his instrument spreading her apart, she groaned loudly, clutching the edge of the island for support. While he bucked her softly against the side of the table, sliding her tits over the smooth granite surface, we watched his muscular buttocks flexing as he pounded her pussy.

It didn't take long for the rest of the group's hands to wander between their legs while they jerked and jilled themselves, moaning in tandem with the sexy couple bent over the kitchen island. As I listened to Madison's escalating moans and gasps, I smiled, knowing she'd captured the ultimate prize.

Maybe that's the way she planned it all along, I thought, slipping three fingers into my dripping pussy, imagining what it would be like to be fucked by Lincoln's baseball-bat-thick firehose. *Two can play that game*, I grunted, determined to get my *own* piece of his organ before the night was over.

9

———

After Madison and Lincoln collected themselves, everybody retired to the kitchen to enjoy some refreshments while they milled around the island, wondering what the next contest would involve. The boys were eager to get back in the game, having been denied a chance to complete the last exercise, but Madison was being elusive about providing any details. Instead, she gorged herself on hors d'oeuvres, licking the tzatziki off her snacks while she stared at Lincoln's dripping instrument with flushed cheeks.

"Don't you think you've had *enough* of him after that last round?" I said, watching her drooling over his buff body.

"I'm not sure you can *ever* have enough of that thing," she grinned, gazing at his big dick. "He never *did* manage to get it all inside of me."

"Yeah, well, you might save a little bit for the *rest* of us girls," I huffed. "There's still six more of us who wouldn't mind having a shot at him."

She paused as she glanced around the table, noticing the other women staring at her enviously.

"Well, at least everybody will have an equal opportunity in the upcoming round. Because in the next contest, it will be the women who are wearing the blindfolds."

"Oh?" Brad said, squeezing in next to us, overhearing the conversation. "Are you going to make the ladies run the gauntlet this time trying to find our waiting cocks?"

"It shouldn't be hard *finding* them," Madison grinned. "The hard part will be determining whose dick belongs to whom."

"With the usual prize for the winner?" Shae said, edging in closer.

"Yes," Maddy nodded. "But in this case, there should be more than one winner. It's starting to getting late, and I don't know how much more stimulation the boys can handle before their dicks begin to fall off. With any luck, *everybody* will have a chance to get off in our grande finale."

"Finale?" Diego said, his ears perking up. "Just when I was starting to get comfortable playing these exotic games. Don't most county fairs close down later than this?"

"Maybe," Madison chuckled. "But never fear, I've got enough ideas for a whole *new* edition of carnival games. I just want to make sure you guys have enough time to recharge your batteries. Because at my *next* party, you're going to need even more strength and stamina to make it through the challenges."

"Mmm, I can't wait," Paige said, joining the group. "Can you at least give us a *hint* about what we can look forward to next time?"

Madison paused when she saw the rest of the group squeezing in around the island, eager to hear about her plans.

"Well, I don't want to give *too* much away," she smiled, darting her eyes around the participants. "But maybe the names I've given some of the contests will give you a bit of an idea. *Firing Range, Kissing Booth, Paint by Numbers, Bobbing for Peaches, and House of Mirrors* are just a few of the games that I've got planned."

"Wow," Lily laughed. "You really *do* stay up late on lonely nights dreaming this stuff up."

"Yes," Madison smiled, intertwining her arms with the others around the table. "Except it's not so lonely when all my friends come over to participate in another round of sexy games."

"So what's this big finale you've got planned?" Marco said, his penis already beginning to flutter at the knowledge it would be the boys' turn to go next.

"Well, since you boys were blindfolded in the last round," Maddy said. "I think it's only fair that we make the *women* work a little harder for the prize this time."

"By being blindfolded, you mean?" Emma said.

"Yes," Madison nodded. "It'll be a bit like our second contest, where the women had to match the flaccid penises with pictures of the men's hard ones. Except in this game that I'm calling Milk the Bull, you'll be doing it purely by *feel*."

Lincoln suddenly cocked his head, widening his eyes.

"You want us to remain *flaccid* while the women are caressing our cocks?" he said.

"God, no," Maddy laughed. "What would be the fun in that? The harder you are, the easier it will be for your partners to guess whose cock it is. Plus, they've had the whole evening to stare at your erect penises while you've participated in each of the exercises. My guess is that it will be a lot easier and quicker for the women to match the erections to the owners when you're fully *aroused*."

"Do we get to choose our partners again?" Laura said, eyeing up Lincoln's lengthening tool with greedy eyes.

"In the interests of fairness, I think the matchups should be by random selection this time. That's the advantage of being blindfolded. Like Brad said earlier, the more variety, the more fun it is."

"Which side of the table will I be sitting on this time?" Shae asked. "Since the ladies will be doing the fondling, I seem to be the odd one out."

"Hmm," Madison said, pinching her eyebrows together as she pondered the predicament. "You're right, with officially six women and six men in the group, being a *transgender* woman, you're kind of the wildcard. It looks like I'll just have to join in the contest once again to even the numbers."

"Then who'll do the *officiating*?" Brad said.

"We'll have to put you on your honor this time," Madison said. "If the women guess you correctly, all you have to do is confirm it verbally."

"Is any other talking allowed?" Diego said.

"I think that would make it too easy to match the men's voices," Madison grinned. "But that shouldn't stop you from *grunting and moaning* all you want."

"How many guesses will each of the women be permitted?" Emma said.

"*Three* should about do it," Madison said. "That will give you at least a fifty-fifty chance of guessing your partner right."

"I think the odds will be a little higher for *some* of the contestants," Bonnie grinned, nodding toward Lincoln's long snake.

"Perhaps so," Maddy nodded. "But the purpose of this contest isn't so much about *winning* as giving everybody a chance for a happy ending."

"And by happy ending," Paige said. "You mean *finishing* our handies?"

"Or however *else* you'd like to satisfy your partner," Madison grinned.

"Including using certain other body parts, if we so desire?" Laura said.

"Absolutely," Maddy smiled. "We did say *everybody*."

10

After Madison finished explaining the contest rules, the men wrapped blindfolds around the women's eyes then they all sat down a few inches apart on the long sectional sofa. When Marco said that the men were ready, the women turned around and groped their way to different areas of the sofa, kneeling in front of their randomly selected partners. By now, the men's flagstaffs were standing straight up awaiting their partner's attention, and the women hummed in excitement after they felt their erect shafts.

When I felt my partner's hard-on, it wasn't immediately apparent who I was touching, since his erection seemed to be of roughly average size with no obvious distinguishing characteristics. But with his crown fully exposed, that narrowed it down to five, remembering that Marco's and Neil's cocks were uncircumcised. And it obviously didn't belong to Lincoln, with his huge, slightly curved cock, or Shae, with her pussy in place of the usual balls. So that only left Brad, Ryan, and Diego.

I rolled my fingers around the tip of my partner's dripping head, and he groaned with a familiar timbre to his voice.

"Mmm," I smiled. "I think I've heard that moan before. Is this *Diego's* pretty cock I've got in my hands?"

"Mmft," my partner grunted, trying to suppress his growing pleasure as I stroked his dick softly with two hands.

"No?" I said, widening my smile while I narrowed the possibilities.

"Maybe *this* might help," I said, cupping his balls with my left hand as I caressed his shaft.

"Uhnn," he groaned, obviously enjoying my two-pronged stimulation of his genitals.

Then I recalled the unique squealing sound that Ryan made when Shae had gripped him from behind while she skewered him with her cock.

"Hmm," I nodded, pulling the tip of his dick down toward my face and releasing it while I listened to it slapping up against his stomach. "I remember this springy dick. Only *Brad's* cock tilts up against his belly like a little boy's. It looks like you've still got plenty of juice left in your batteries."

"You have an unfair advantage," Brad grunted while I fondled his balls and stroked his dick gently. "You've already *felt* my balls and cock during the candy floss contest."

"Yes, but that was mostly with my *mouth*," I grinned, rolling my tongue around the sides of my lips.

"There's no one stopping you from using that to full advantage now," he panted. "Madison said you could use any part of your body to stimulate us after you identified your partner."

"True," I grinned, squeezing his dick harder in my hands. "But I think I'll make you wait a little longer until we see how many of the other contestants guess their partners."

Suddenly, I heard the woman next to me chuckle as she nudged her hips softly against me.

"I guess that rules my *husband* out," Laura said while her partner groaned and huffed a few feet over her head. "As if I needed any help figuring *that* one out. So, using Jade's reasoning, that means this is either Diego or Ryan, since I can tell you're obviously cut."

She paused for a moment while I heard her shift position between her partner's legs as he moaned softly above her.

"But I remember Ryan makes a unique sound when his balls are squeezed. Is that *you*, Ryan?"

Her partner huffed and grunted, trying to suppress his pleasure while Laura teased his balls, then she leaned back, nodding triumphantly.

"Mmm, I *thought* it might be you, Diego," she purred. "Your cock is so smooth and straight. It's *burning* in my hands."

"Yes," he panted. "Stroke me with both hands. I want to watch my cock pumping in and out of your fists."

"Fuck, yes," Laura hissed, raising her voice to make her husband more jealous, who was huffing along with Diego while I stroked him in kind.

One by one, the women sitting opposite their partners narrowed down the field of candidates as they listened to the others reveal their identities, until there were only two contestants left. Lincoln was the first to be identified by Paige, who was kneeling on my opposite side, then Shae was quickly tagged by her partner Madison, who immediately recognized the transgender girl when she felt her dripping pussy under her flaring cock. That left only Marco and Neil, but with three guesses each, their partners quickly narrowed down the choices to the correct owners after pulling on their tight foreskins.

I smiled when I realized how Madison had formulated this contest to be easily won by all of the candidates, and as I listened to the men moaning in unison while their partners jerked their cocks between their legs, I flipped off my bandana and glanced down the line. It was a beautiful sight watching the look of pleasure on the men's faces while they stared at the women stroking their hard-ons with single-minded purpose, but I was eager to finish up this contest with a flourish.

"Screw this *jerking off* business," I said out loud. "I'm taking matters into my own hands before we turn the lights out for the night. What do you say, ladies? Madison said we could finish this contest any way we wanted. I don't know about you girls, but I plan on finishing with my *own* a happy ending along with the rest of the guys. Let's ditch these bandanas and enjoy this last game as a united group!"

"You took the words right out of my mouth, Jade," Madison said, ripping off her bandana and staring at Shae's throbbing hard-on and dripping pussy with wide eyes. Let's give our partners something truly memorable to take away with them before they leave the party. Let's see who can come the hardest and the quickest!"

"Damn straight," I nodded, standing up and flipping around to lower my pussy over Brad's bobbing organ. "That is, if you don't mind my availing myself of your husband's perky penis, Laura."

"Of course not," Laura said, following my lead and squatting down over Diego's erection, facing away. "Why do you think we came to this party anyway? To keep having boring sex only with our *own* partners?"

"I wouldn't exactly call it bor–" Brad protested before

being drowned out by Paige's loud moan as she planted her thick butt over Lincoln's tall tool.

Within seconds, all of the women had impaled themselves over their partner's dicks, bouncing happily up and down while they peered at one another with glassy eyes and gaping mouths, groaning in delirious pleasure. While they played with their tits with one hand and squeezed their partners' balls with their other, I glanced to the other end of the sofa watching Madison's face beginning to flush as she thrust three fingers into Shae's gaping hole while she bounced her hips over her flexing hard-on.

It didn't take long for everybody to begin screaming and howling in mutual ecstasy while the women rode their partners' cocks together in the reverse cowgirl position, whooping and hollering like a band of drunken schoolgirls.

Country fair, indeed, I smiled as I felt my climax wash over me with the rest of the group. *Except in this one, everyone's a winner.*

READY FOR MORE EROTIC *chills and thrills? Order the next exciting volume in the Carny Games trilogy, Carny Games 2. Buy direct and save at victoriarusherotica. Or download from your favorite online bookstore here: retailer links.*

*These carnival games require a whole different kind of
skill...*

ALSO BY VICTORIA RUSH

Adult Fairytales:

The Enchanted Forest: An Erotic Fairytale

The Land of Giants: An Erotic Fairytale

The Dragon's Lair: An Erotic Fairytale

Witch's Brew: An Erotic Fairytale

The Mage's Spell: An Erotic Fairytale

The Mermaid Lagoon: An Erotic Fairytale

The Coven: An Erotic Fairytale

Rapunzel: An Erotic Fairytale

The Seven Dwarfs: An Erotic Fairytale

The Land of Mutants: An Erotic Fairytale

The Erotic Temple: A Sexy Fairytale (Coming Soon)

Erotica Themed Bundles:

Voyeur: Lesbian Erotica Bundle

Public Affairs: A Lesbian Anthology

Futa Fantasies: The Ladyboy Collection

Threesomes: The Lesbian Collection

Threesomes - Volume 2: The Lesbian Collection

First Time: A Lesbian Anthology

Hedonism: An Erotic Anthology

Switch Hitters: Bisexual Erotica

Taboo Erotica: The Lesbian Series

BDSM: The Lesbian Collection

Party Games: The Erotic Collection

Party Games 2: The Erotic Collection

All Girl 1: Lesbian Erotica Bundle

All Girl 2: Lesbian Erotica Bundle

All Girl 3: Lesbian Erotica Bundle

All Girl 4: Lesbian Erotica Bundle

Erotic Fairytale Bundles:

Clover's Fantasy Adventures: Books 1 - 5

Clover's Fantasy Adventures: Books 6 - 10

Erotic Fantasy:

Pirate's Bounty: A Time Travel Adventure

Wild West: A Time Travel Adventure

Private Riley: A Time Travel Adventure

Cleopatra's Secret: A Time Travel Adventure

Bounty Hunter 2125: A Time Travel Adventure

Ninja Assassin: A Time Travel Adventure

The 300: A Time Travel Adventure

Arabian Nights: An Erotic Fairytale (coming soon...)

Steamy Time Travel Bundles:

Riley's Time Travel Adventures: Books 1 - 5

Lesbian Erotica:

The Dinner Party: Lesbian Voyeur Erotica

The Darkroom: Bisexual Voyeur Erotica

Naked Yoga: Lesbian Transgender Erotica

Nude Cruise: Bisexual Voyeur Erotica

Rush Hour: Taboo Public Sex

The Girl Next Door: First Time Lesbian Erotic Romance

Girls' Camp: Lesbian Group Sex

Wet Dream: Ladyboy Fantasy Erotica

The Convent: Taboo Sex with a Nun

Sex Robot: A Dream Sex Machine

The Personal Trainer: Getting Pumped at the Gym

The Dominatrix: BDSM Lesbian Domination

Webcam Chat: Lesbian Online Sex

Paint Me: A Kinky Bodypainting Workshop

The Toy Party: Girls Sharing Sex Toys

The Costume Party: Strapping One On

Swedish Sauna: Lesbian Group Sex

The Therapist: Taboo Lesbian Erotica

Elevator Shaft: Bisexual Threesomes Erotica

Ladyboy: Lesbian Transgender Erotica

Peep Show: Lesbian Voyeur Erotica

The Dare: Public Sex Erotica

Maid Service: Lesbian Threesomes Erotica

The Hitchhiker: First Time Lesbian Erotica

The Housesitter: Spycam Lesbian Erotica

The Spa: Lesbian Group Orgy

Parlor Games: Blindfold Sex Party

The Exchange Student: First Time Lesbian Erotica

The Hostel: Bisexual Group Erotica

The Harem: Lesbian Erotic Romance

The Orient Express: Lesbian Voyeur Erotica

The First Lady: A Forbidden Lesbian Erotic Romance

The Slave: Lesbian BDSM Erotica

The Masseuse: Lesbian Sensuous Erotica

Too Close for Comfort: Lesbian Forbidden Erotica

Naked Twister: A Wild Party Game

Lexi: The Sex App (Lesbian Fantasy Erotica)

Call Girl: Lesbian Bisexual Threesomes Erotica

Circle Jill: Lesbian Masturbation Workshop

The Viewing Room: Masturbation Voyeur Erotica

Spin the Bottle: A Kinky Party Game

The Hair Salon: Lesbian Voyeur Erotica

Tribadism 1: Girls Only Sex Workshop

Tribadism 2: The Art of Scissoring

Tribadism 3: Threeway Hookups

The Kiss: A Game of Oral Sex

Pledge Week: Sorority Sisters

Carny Games 1: A Wild Sex Party

Carny Games 2: A Kinky Sex Party

Carny Games 3: An Erotic Sex Party

Dreamscape: An Artificial Reality Game

Glory Hole: Guess Who's On the Other Side

Joy Ride: A Late Night Erotic Bus Trip

The Blind Girl: An Erotic Romance(Coming Soon)

Lesbian Erotica Bundles:

Jade's Erotic Adventures: Books 1 - 5

Jade's Erotic Adventures: Books 6 - 10

Jade's Erotic Adventures: Books 11 - 15

Jade's Erotic Adventures: Books 16 - 20

Jade's Erotic Adventures: Books 21 - 25

Jade's Erotic Adventures: Books 26 - 30

Jade's Erotic Adventures: Books 31 - 35

Jade's Erotic Adventures: Books 36 - 40

Jade's Erotic Adventures: Books 41 - 45

Jade's Erotic Adventures: Books 46 - 50

Fifty Shades of Jade: Superbundle

Standalone Stories:

The Polynesian Girl: A Lesbian EroticRomance

FOLLOW VICTORIA RUSH:

Want to keep informed of my latest erotic book releases? Sign up for my newsletter and receive a FREE bonus book:

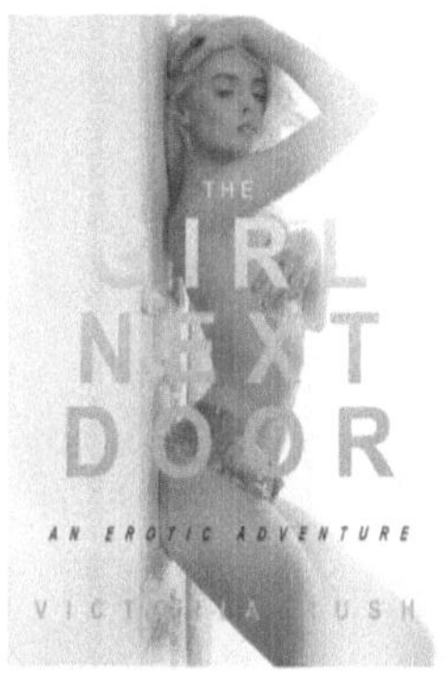

Spying on the neighbors just got a lot more interesting...